Knoc... Knock!

Written by Dominic Butters
Illustrated by Fabio Santomauro

Collins

Joe was expecting a visitor.
He was waiting for
his friend Harry.

Knock! Knock!
Joe shot up and opened the door,
but it wasn't Harry. It was ...

... a POLAR BEAR!
His iceberg had melted,
so Joe gave him an ice lolly
and sent him on his way.

Joe went back to wait for Harry.

Knock! Knock!
Joe jumped up and opened the door,
but it wasn't Harry. It was ...

... an ALIEN! His spaceship had run out of fuel and had crash-landed on the front lawn.

So Joe gave him some batteries and sent him on his way.

Joe went back to wait for Harry.
Knock! Knock!
Joe slowly got out of his chair to open the door, but it wasn't Harry. It was …

... a PIRATE!
His ship had capsized,
so Joe gave him his toy ship
and sent him on his way.

Joe went back to wait for Harry.

Knock! Knock!
Joe crawled to the door. It was ...

11

... Harry!
But Joe was too tired to play.

Knocking at the door

Ideas for reading

Written by Linda Pagett B.Ed (hons), M.Ed
Lecturer and Educational Consultant

Learning objectives: recognise and use alternative ways of pronouncing the graphemes already taught; explore the effect of patterns of language; act out their own stories, using voices for characters; create simple texts that combine words and pictures; use capital letters and full stops

Curriculum links: Citizenship: Choices

High frequency words: was, his, had, so, him, but, out, some, got, back, too

Interest words: polar bear, iceberg, alien, spaceship, batteries, pirate, capsized, crawled

Resources: whiteboard, pen and paper

Word count: 174

Getting started

- Introduce the story by reading the front and back covers together and encouraging children to predict who is knocking at the door.

- Encourage children to think of other stories and poems where someone knocks at the door e.g. *The Three Little Pigs.*

- Explain that *knock* has a silent letter *k* and write other examples on the whiteboard, e.g. knee, knife, knit. Encourage children to segment sounds in order to read and spell these words for themselves.

Reading and responding

- Encourage children to read independently from the beginning, drawing their attention to the words that are followed by an exclamation mark and how they are emphasised.

- Listen to each child read in turn, prompting and praising for using the pictures, context and phonic cues to support them.

- Ask questions related to meaning as children read, e.g. *Why do you think the pirate's ship capsized? What do you think Harry did when Joe was too tired to play?*